On the Red World

LEO P. KELLEY

A Pacemaker® Book

Fearon Education
a division of
David S. Lake Publishers
Belmont, California

Series Director: Robert G. Bander
Designer: Richard Kharibian
Cover and illustrations: Rick Guidice

ISBN–0–8224–3202–1
Library of Congress Catalog Card Number: 78–68227
Printed in the United States of America.

1. 9 8 7 6 5

CONTENTS

CHAPTER 1

TO THE RED WORLD

Far from Earth, the spaceship Voyager flew through outer space. It made no sound because there was no air in space to carry sound. All around the ship were stars and planets. Voyager flew past one planet that had two moons in orbit around it.

Inside the ship, Steve Estrada was sleeping. He didn't hear the signal that came through the ship's control board. He didn't hear the man's voice that said:

"If any ship can hear my signal, please answer me. I'm in trouble and I need help. Over."

1

Some time later, Steve woke up. He got out of bed and put on his clothes. Then he left his room and climbed down the steps to the bottom of the ship. He went into the control room. No signal came through the control board now.

Steve checked the control room. On the big video screens above the control board, he could see many stars and planets. Then he checked the control board. Green lights showed that Voyager was right on course.

As he walked through the ship, he met Ellen Drake. She was up early, checking to be sure that everything was in order. She tested all the air locks. They were fine. She checked to be sure that the air supply was OK. It was. She also checked each of the ship's laser guns.

Steve walked on through the ship. He felt as if it had been made for him and he had been made for it. It was a good feeling. Steve thought of himself as a lucky person. How many other people had everything they wanted in life? Not many, he knew. But *he* had what he wanted—a ship in which he could sail between the stars. And a life which, for him, was better than any he could live on Earth.

"Good morning, Voyager," he said to the ship.

Voyager answered him at once in its clear voice. "GOOD MORNING, ESTRADA. I SHOULD TELL YOU THAT WE GOT A SIGNAL SOME TIME AGO."

"Who was it from?"

Voyager answered, "THE MAN WHO CALLED DID NOT GIVE HIS NAME."

"Maybe he'll call back," Steve said and then he asked, "Where's Drake now?"

"AT THE TOP OF THE SHIP. SOON I WILL HAVE BREAKFAST READY FOR YOU BOTH."

Steve climbed to the top part of the ship. There he found Ellen on the floor doing push-ups.

"Hello, Estrada," she said, as he came into the room. "Why don't you join me in some exercise before breakfast?"

"Good idea." Steve fell to the floor and began to do some push-ups. So did Ellen. After the push-ups they both did some sit-ups.

Voyager spoke to them during their exercise. "I CAN HELP YOU WITH YOUR EXERCISE."

"How?" Ellen asked.

"I CAN MAKE THE FORCE OF GRAVITY STRONGER IN HERE. IF I DO THAT, YOU WILL HAVE TO WORK VERY HARD AT YOUR

EXERCISE. BUT IT WILL BE GOOD FOR
YOU. IT WILL HELP YOU KEEP IN THE
BEST SHAPE."

"Good idea, Voyager," Steve said. "Do it."

Almost at once, Steve felt heavy. He found it
hard to walk. It was hard to move even a little

bit. "OK, Voyager," he said. "That's enough. Leave the force of gravity the way you've got it now. Any more and I couldn't move a finger."

Ellen reached down to touch her toes. That wasn't too hard. But to get up again—*that* was hard. But she kept at the exercise.

So did Steve. He did some more push-ups and then some more sit-ups.

When they had both finished their exercise, Steve spoke to Voyager. "Please return the force of gravity to what it was."

Voyager did so at once. Steve felt as if a great stone had been lifted from his back.

"I'm *really* hungry now," Ellen said. "That exercise has made me so hungry I could eat a dozen eggs!"

Voyager said, "I AM SORRY, BUT YOU WILL NOT HAVE A DOZEN EGGS FOR BREAK-FAST. INSTEAD, YOU WILL EACH HAVE TWO EGGS, BREAD, AND MILK. HOPE YOU WILL FIND THEM GOOD."

Ellen laughed. She couldn't stop laughing for a minute. When she did finally stop, she said, "Voyager is just too much sometimes."

"I know what you mean," Steve said. "Voyager thinks we mean everything we say."

Ellen laughed again.

Then the ship gave them their breakfast. The food came out of a little glass box in the wall of the room.

Ellen tasted it. "It's good," she said to Steve.

"Very good," he said.

As they ate, they talked. Ellen said she wished they were already on Planet 1 of Star 84 in Galaxy 5.

"But we won't get there for a long time yet," Steve said. "It will take us many more light years to reach Galaxy 5."

"I wonder what it will really be like there," Ellen said as she drank some milk.

Steve said, "Very different from Earth."

"That will make it fun, won't it?" Ellen asked, smiling.

"I'm not sure that it will be fun. I *am* sure it will be a lot of very hard work to build our Earth Colony there."

"You know something," Ellen said. "You and I are very different. You often see the dark side of things. I like to look at the bright side."

"Sorry. I can't help it. It's just the way I am, I guess."

"Don't get me wrong, Steve. I didn't mean

your way of seeing things was bad. Just different, that's all."

Ellen finished the last of her breakfast and stood up. "I think I'll check our star maps. I want to check just how far we have to go before we reach New World City. Everything is ready for the supply stop there. After we give them the things we have on board for them, then we move on to Galaxy 5."

Steve got up. He followed Ellen out of the room and down the steps to the control room.

Ellen checked her star map. "Galaxy 5 is still so far away." She then checked the facts on the planet they were headed for.

"New World City is on a really small planet," she said. "Look, Estrada." She pointed to the place on the map that gave the facts about the planet.

Steve read them out loud:

" . . . *and the planet's sun is red. That is why some astronauts call the planet 'the red world.' The planet does not turn on its axis. It simply moves around its red sun without turning. Because it does not turn on its axis, the planet has a day side and a night side.*"

Steve stopped reading. "Interesting," he said. "I wonder what it would be like to live in a place where it is always day."

"Or where it is always night. I don't think I'd like to live on the night side. I'd rather live on the day side."

Steve pushed a button on the control board. A small screen grew bright in front of him. There were words on the screen. They told him that New World City was four years old. Many hundreds of people lived there. They had come from almost every country on Earth. New World City had been the first Earth Colony in outer space.

"How soon will we get to the planet, Voyager?" he asked.

"WE ARE ALMOST THERE NOW," the ship answered.

"I'll signal them," Ellen said. She sat down in front of the control board. "We should let them know that we're on our way. We don't want to just drop in on them. That wouldn't be nice, would it, Estrada?"

"I don't think it matters, Drake."

Ellen laughed. "You're almost cool, Estrada!"

Steve smiled. Ellen turned on the signal system. "New World City, this is the spaceship Voyager calling. Do you read me? Come in, New World City. Over."

She waited. No answer.

She signaled again. "Spaceship Voyager to New World City. Come in, please. Over."

Still no answer.

She looked up at Steve. She was about to say something to him. Just then, a man's voice came over the signal system.

"Hello, Voyager. This is New World City. We read you. Over."

"Hello, there," Ellen said. "I thought something was wrong when you didn't answer right away."

"Something *is* wrong here, Voyager. It happened yesterday. I have to tell you that you're in for trouble if you land here. But we need your help."

"What happened?" Steve asked. "Who are you?"

"My name is Don Chadrow. I called before but got no answer. Wait a minute. I think something is. . . . Can you hold, Voyager?"

"We can hold," Ellen said. She looked at

Steve. But she didn't say anything. They waited. Several minutes passed. Ellen couldn't stand the wait any longer. "Don Chadrow in New World City—do you read me? Over."

The sound of a loud crash came through the signal system.

"Chadrow!" Steve yelled. "What . . . ?"

Don Chadrow's voice came to them again. Now it was weak. "They are trying to break in here. I've got to. . . ."

There was a second crash. Ellen couldn't reach Chadrow. He didn't answer her call. She stood up and gave orders to Voyager.

At once, the ship went into orbit around the planet.

CHAPTER **2**

NEW WORLD CITY

Voyager didn't stay long in orbit. It circled the planet only once. Then it landed near New World City.

Ellen looked up at the video screen. On it was a picture of the city. Its buildings were tall and flags flew from the tops of some of them. All the buildings sat in the warm, red light of the sun far above them.

"The red world," Ellen said. Then, to Steve she said, "Everything looks OK out there. But

I wonder what was breaking in on Don Chadrow."

Steve was looking at the video screens. "That's some city, isn't it?"

"It's beautiful. It's like no city on Earth. It looks like a dream."

"Well," Steve said, "Out we go, right?"

Ellen looked at him. "We have to. Chadrow is in danger."

"But you don't really want to go, do you?"

"I do and I don't," Ellen said. "But what *I* want isn't the important thing. To help the people is. Let's go, Estrada."

Steve said, "The air out there is almost like the air on Earth. So we'll be OK."

"Let's take our laser guns," Ellen said.

They got their laser guns. Then they went through the ship's air lock and down the steps outside the ship.

Ellen looked up at the red sun in the sky. "It's strange, isn't it? That sun makes this world look as if it's on fire."

Steve looked from side to side. They were in an open field. Nothing grew in the field.

"I don't see any people," he said.

"Maybe they're all inside the city." Ellen started to walk toward it.

Steve caught up with her. They met no one on their way.

When they reached the city, Ellen's hand closed upon her laser gun. They had not gone very far into the city when they heard a loud noise. It was the sound of glass breaking. At the same time, they heard a man scream. They both stopped and looked at one another.

"I wonder . . ." Ellen said. She pointed down the street.

A man had just turned the corner and was coming toward them. He was running but not very fast. He fell against one of the buildings. Then he began to run again.

"Come on," Ellen said to Steve. "That man looks like he's been hurt. Let's see if we can help him."

She and Steve ran toward the man. Just as they reached him, he fell down at their feet.

Steve picked him up and helped him sit with his back against a wall. "What's wrong? What's happened to you?"

The man's clothes were torn. There was blood on his face and on his hands. He tried to answer Steve's question, but he couldn't seem to speak. His eyes were wide, and his whole body shook.

"Take it easy," Ellen said to him. "We'll help you. We'll take you back to our ship and. . . ."

The man shook his head. "Too late," he whispered. "I'm done for. I know it. They got me, and they. . . ."

The man fell over.

"Estrada!" Ellen said. "Hold him up."

"It's no use, Drake," Steve said. "He's dead."

"But what happened to him?"

"Nothing good." Steve went inside one of the buildings. Ellen came in behind him. They looked around. There were no people in the building. Only broken chairs and tables. Lamps had been smashed and lay on the floor in pieces.

They left the building and went into the one next door. There they found the same thing. Everything had been smashed. And there were no people to be seen.

But on the next block, they found some people. All of them were dead. There was a woman and several men. There was also a little boy.

"I don't think I can take seeing any more of this," Steve said. "Let's go back to Voyager. We can try to get through to Don Chadrow again."

"Good idea," Ellen said. "We've got to find out what happened here. He can probably tell us *if* we can get through to him."

They started back toward the ship. But they had not gone far when they came upon some robots.

There were six robots. All of them were coming toward Steve and Ellen. They were made of metal. The red light of the sun made the metal shine. Each robot had only three fingers on each hand. Each had only one eye.

When the robots saw Ellen and Steve, they stopped for a minute. Then they began to run toward them.

"Now maybe we'll get some answers," Steve said. "We can ask these robots what happened here." He went to meet the robots.

When he reached them, one of the robots hit him hard with its metal hand. Steve let out a yell. He fell back and then hit the ground.

Ellen ran up to him. She stood over him with her laser gun in her hand.

"Don't move," she told the robots. "Stand right where you are."

But the robots acted as if they had not heard her. One reached out to grab her gun.

She ducked to one side. "Estrada!" she yelled. "Can you get up?"

Steve got to his feet. One of the robots made a grab for him. He gave it a kick. His kick sent the robot flying back. It banged into the robot behind it. Both of them went down.

"Ellen!" Steve shouted. "Look out!"

Ellen turned around fast. She saw the robot behind her and fired her laser gun at it. The robot broke into several pieces. Wires flew through the air.

"Run!" Ellen yelled to Steve.

They both ran. But the robots ran after them.

Ellen looked back. "They're faster than we are. In a minute, they're going to catch up with us."

Steve looked around as he ran. Then he saw it. Off to one side was a place where many helicars were parked. Near the helicars was a big drum of oil.

"Drake, head for those helicars!" he yelled.

When they reached them, Steve ran behind the big drum of oil. Several seconds later, they were able to turn it over. The oil poured out of the drum and ran down the street toward the robots.

Steve fired his laser gun at the spilled oil. The flash of light from his gun hit the oil in the street. It began to burn. The robots stopped. The fire kept them from coming down the street toward Steve and Ellen.

"That fire won't burn for very long," Ellen said.

"So let's take to the sky," Steve said with a big smile.

"What do you mean?"

"We'll take one of these helicars and fly back to Voyager."

Steve ran to the nearest one and got in. But he got right back out again. "It's out of order," he told Ellen. "This must be a place where they fix helicars."

"Maybe we can find one that's already been fixed." Ellen ran over to one of the other helicars. "Here's one that will fly!" She yelled to Steve and got into it.

Steve joined her and climbed in beside her. He turned on the helicar's motor. Its wings began to move. Then it lifted itself off the ground.

But at the same time, several robots ran through the fire that was almost all burned out. One of them made a grab for the helicar and caught one of its wings. The helicar turned on its side.

Steve tried to hold on but he couldn't. He fell out of the helicar. Ellen jumped out of the other side of the helicar when she saw him fall.

She raced to where he was and helped him up. Then they both began to run again.

"This way!" Ellen yelled. "We can circle around these buildings and. . . ."

An idea hit her. She grabbed Steve's hand and pulled him into one of the buildings.

"Where are we going now?" he asked her.

"Maybe we can find a way to cut through this building to the street on the other side. The robots won't know which building we're in. By the time they find out, we'll be out of the city, if we're lucky."

The two humans ran through the building. Finally they found its back door. They ran through the door and out into another street. Then they raced for the gate of the city.

They met no more robots. Soon they were through the gate and close to Voyager.

Then they heard the sound of laser guns firing near the ship.

CHAPTER 3

THE FORCE FIELD

"Those robots didn't have laser guns," Ellen shouted.

They ran on. When they were near Voyager, they found out it was Voyager firing the laser guns. The ship was firing its guns at a group of robots who were trying to get inside.

"Good old Voyager!" Ellen said as she stopped running.

"Take cover," Steve said. "We don't want those robots to come after us."

"Maybe Voyager will be able to destroy

them all," Ellen said as she and Steve took cover behind some red trees.

A robot blew up as one of Voyager's laser guns hit it. But soon Steve and Ellen saw that Voyager was going to lose the fight. There were too many robots. They were all over the ship.

"Look, Estrada!" Ellen said. "There are robots on the steps. They're trying to break in."

"Voyager can't hit them there. We'd better do something fast!"

"I'm going to try to draw the fire of the robots," Ellen shouted. "I'll go over there and then I'll fire at them. They'll come after me. When they do, you make a run for the ship. Once you get inside, order Voyager to set up a force field to keep the robots away."

"That's no good," Steve said. "If I do get into the ship and Voyager sets up a force field, it will keep you out of the ship as well as the robots."

"Don't worry about that now. I'll take care of myself—and those robots." But Ellen really didn't believe her own words. She just wanted to be sure that Estrada believed them.

"I think we'd better stick together," Steve said. "I'd hate to see them trap you."

"No," Ellen said. "Get to the ship if you can."

She didn't give Steve time to say anything more. She ran out of the trees. Then she turned and fired her laser gun. She just missed one of the robots.

At the sound of her gun, they all turned from the ship. When they saw her, they charged.

She fired again. And again. She hit one of the robots. But the others all kept coming.

When all the robots had left the ship, Steve ran toward it. He raced up the steps and opened the door.

Once inside the ship, he said, "Voyager, Drake is out there. We've got to try to save her." Steve got behind one of the ship's laser guns. He said nothing to Voyager about setting up a force field.

Voyager said, "I DID NOT SEE THE RO-BOTS COMING. IF I HAD, I COULD HAVE SET UP A FORCE FIELD TO KEEP THEM AWAY. BUT THEY GOT TOO CLOSE TO ME BEFORE I SAW THEM."

Steve fired his laser gun. "Shoot, Voyager!" he said. "But be careful! Don't hit Drake."

Voyager fired several times. He hit a group of several robots. All of them blew up.

When Ellen saw what had happened, she began to run toward the ship.

Steve fired to cover her as she ran. "Voyager," he said, "keep firing. I'm going to the door." He ran to the door, opened it, and Ellen ran up the steps and into the ship.

Steve shut the door and locked it. "Voyager,"

he said, *"now's* the time for the force field. *Quick!* Set it up before those robots get any closer to us."

Suddenly there was a soft sound in the ship. The sound grew louder. Then it stopped.

"THE FORCE FIELD IS NOW IN PLACE," Voyager said. "NOW WE ARE SAFE FROM THE ROBOTS."

Steve and Ellen watched the robots through the ship's windows. They ran into the force field which they couldn't see. But it was there— all around Voyager.

The robots couldn't get past it. As they ran into it, they fell down. The force field didn't hurt them. But it kept them away from the ship. It was as if there was a wall around Voyager. A wall that no one could see.

Voyager said, "WHILE YOU WERE GONE, I GOT A SIGNAL."

"Who sent it?" Steve asked.

"HIS NAME WAS DON CHADROW. HE SAID YOU SHOULD RETURN HIS SIGNAL AS SOON AS POSSIBLE."

Ellen turned on the signal system. "This is Voyager calling Don Chadrow. Do you read me? Come in, please. Over."

"Am I glad to hear you, Voyager!" It was the voice of Don Chadrow. It sounded weak. "I was waiting for you to signal. I couldn't have waited much longer."

Ellen told him that she and Steve had just been inside the city. She told him about the robots. She asked him again what had happened in the city.

"I haven't got time to tell you now," Don said. "I've got to get out of here. The robots almost got me before. They ran off to attack your spaceship. But they will be back. I know they will."

"What can we do to help you?" Steve asked.

"I'm leaving here now," Don said. "I've got my helicar up on the roof of this building. I think I can get to it now before the robots get back. With a little luck, I'll take off. When you see my helicar, you'll know I got away. Then you lift off and meet me on the night side of the planet."

Don then told them where to meet him and how to find the spot. The last thing he said was, "Then I'll tell you all about the trouble."

Ellen turned off the signal system. Then she watched the robots on the small video screen.

The robots were still trying to get past the force field. But they couldn't.

A few minutes later, she saw a helicar leave the roof of a building in the city. Its four wings were on top of its round body. The wir.gs turned so fast they they couldn't be seen when the helicar was in the air. The helicar flew up into the sky and was gone.

Steve gave orders to Voyager. The spaceship lifted off and set a course for the night side of the little planet.

CHAPTER **4**

AT THE CAMP

Inside the ship, Ellen was busy at the control board. Steve watched the video screens. In a few minutes, he saw what he had hoped to see. The screens showed a picture of a big fire.

"Drake," he said, "we are now over the camp that Chadrow told us about."

"Voyager," Ellen said, "land near the camp fire."

When the ship was on the ground, Steve and Ellen left it.

People were coming toward them.

"Hello there!" a woman called out to them. She held her head high and seemed very sure of herself.

Steve and Ellen waved to her. As she came up to them, all the other people began to talk. Everyone talked at once. The woman asked them not to talk for a minute.

Then she said, "My name is Ruth Chadrow. I'm very glad to see you. You're the people Don was waiting for."

"We talked to him," Ellen said.

Ruth let out a cry of joy. "Then he is safe?"

"Yes," Steve said. "He is as far as we know. Right now he's on his way here in a helicar."

"Oh, I'm so glad," Ruth said. "I begged him not to stay in the city. I was afraid the robots would kill him. But he said he had to stay. He wanted to signal you when you came."

"Well, he did," Ellen said. "That's why we're here. He told us to meet him here. A minute ago you said your name was Chadrow. Are you Don's sister?"

Ruth shook her head and smiled. "No, I'm his wife. Don and I were married four years ago just before we both came here. We knew each other on Earth. We grew up together there."

"What's that noise?" Steve asked. But before anyone could answer him, he knew what was making the noise. "That's the sound of a heli-car," he said. "That must be Don."

It was. The helicar flew into sight above the fire. It circled the fire and then landed near it. Don got out of his helicar. He was a husky man with bright eyes.

Ruth ran to meet him. They kissed. Then, arm in arm, they walked back to the group of people.

"I'm Don Chadrow," Don said as he gave Steve a firm handshake.

"I'm Steve Estrada. This is Ellen Drake," Steve said. "We are all lucky to be alive."

Ellen shook hands with Don.

"You have already met my wife, haven't you?"

"Yes, we have," Ellen said. Then she asked Don to tell her what had happened in the city.

Don sat down by the fire. Ruth sat down next to him. Steve and Ellen also sat down.

The other people took places by the fire.

Don told them about the city and about the robots. He said that the robots were helpers in New World City. They were controlled by a very small computer. The computer was placed inside a man's head. The man was the leader of the city. The computer had been connected to his brain.

But the man was dead. He had been killed in a helicar crash only yesterday.

After the crash when the man died, the robots went out of control. The computer had controlled them. But it didn't now. The robots, Don explained, went wild. They broke into buildings. They smashed things. They killed people.

Some people in the city escaped to the night side of the planet.

"But what if the robots find you here?" Ellen asked.

It was Ruth who answered her question. "The robots won't come here. They can't see here. They were made to be able to see in the light of our red sun over on the day side. So we're safe here."

"But," Don said, "we can't stay here. We have to go back to the city. And that means that we have to bring the robots under our control once again."

"Couldn't you destroy them with laser guns?" Steve asked.

"Maybe we could," Don said. "But there are probably too many of them. There is only one way to really do this."

He said that the only way was to use a special computer. With it, the robots would be brought under control. But the computer had to be connected to a living person's brain. It wouldn't work any other way. He had decided, Don said, to have the computer connected to his brain.

Ruth spoke up then. "That's because Don is the only one who will do it."

"Ruth isn't very happy about the idea," Don said. "But she understands that I must do it. It's for the good of all of us."

"Do you have the computer here?" Steve asked.

Don said he did. He asked Ruth to get it. She left the fire and returned with the computer. She held it in her hand. She showed it to Steve

and Ellen. It wasn't even as big as a penny.

Ellen said, "Do you mean that tiny computer can control all those robots?"

"Yes, it can," Don said. "But not until it's connected to a human brain—*my* brain this time."

Ruth looked away.

"You'll need a doctor to do that, won't you?" Steve asked. "Do you have a doctor in your group?"

Don smiled. "We have a very good doctor in our group. The best. You have already met her."

Ellen was pleased. "Ruth, how long have you been a doctor?"

Ruth was looking into the fire. In a low voice, she said, "For three years now. I know how to do this. I can connect the computer to Don's brain."

Don put his arms around her. He spoke to her in a whisper, but Steve and Ellen heard what he said.

"Remember what you said yesterday?"

"I remember," Ruth said.

"You said you know the operation will not change me into a computer. You said I will still be the man you love. Do you really believe this is true, Ruth?"

"Yes, I do," Ruth said. "It's just the idea that you will have this new power—over those *things*. It's . . . strange."

"Your husband has always been a little strange, my dear," Don whispered. "Now you know that's true, don't you?"

Ruth couldn't help herself. She had to laugh. "You're not strange, Don. You are a very brave man, and I love you for it."

"Then you'll do it?"

"I will."

Don pulled Ruth close to him and turned to Steve and Ellen. "Now comes the really hard part."

"You can't do the operation here, can you, Ruth?" Ellen asked.

Ruth shook her head. "No. I can't. That's what Don means about the hard part. We'll have to go into the city—to the hospital there."

"But the robots. . . ." Steve said.

"I know," Don said. "It will be dangerous with them around. But we have to go."

Don began to explain his plan for getting to the hospital. It wouldn't be easy, he said. But it might work out. Would Steve and Ellen be interested in helping with the plan?

They said they would be.

Then Steve had an idea. He turned to Ellen. "You fly Voyager back to the day side, Drake. Land near the city. When the robots see Voyager, they will try to get into the ship. Set up another force field. That way you'll be safe. But you'll keep the robots busy and away from the hospital."

"That's a fine idea!" Don said.

"I'd better leave first," Ellen said. "It will take your helicar longer to get there, Don. By the time you get to the city, I'll be keeping the robots busy."

"Right," Don said. "You go first and then we'll follow in a little while. The three of us can just about fit into my helicar."

Ellen stood up. Steve walked with her to Voyager. Just before she got on board, she said, "I'll be safe inside Voyager. But you won't be safe out there in the city, Estrada. So be careful. You will be careful, won't you?"

"I'll be as careful as I can. See you later."

Steve watched her climb into the ship. Then he stepped back. When the ship with its jets full of fire flew up into the sky, he returned to the camp.

"Ruth and I are ready," Don told him when he got there.

"So am I," Steve said. "I'm as ready as I'll ever be."

They said good-bye to the others. People wished them luck. Then the three of them got into Don's helicar. The helicar's wings began to move. And then it rose into the dark that was all around it.

CHAPTER **5**

TRAPPED!

For the three people in the helicar, it was night one minute, and the next minute it was day. They flew over the day side of the planet. Soon New World City came into sight.

Don sat at the helicar's controls. They circled the city.

"There it is," Steve said. "Over there."

Voyager had landed. The ship sat almost a mile from the city. The robots were moving toward Voyager. The helicar followed them.

When the robots got near the ship, they were

stopped by the force field Ellen had set up. They couldn't get past it. Some of them began to pound on it. Others threw stones at it. But the force field held.

Don turned the helicar around and flew back over the city. He landed on the roof of the hospital. Everyone got out of the helicar. Then they ran down the steps, Ruth in the lead.

She led them to the operating room and began at once to get ready for the operation. She put on a white gown after she had washed her hands and put on rubber gloves. Then she put a piece of white cloth over her hair. She used another one to cover her mouth and nose.

She took out the many things she would need for the operation. As Steve looked at them he remembered that when he was a kid he had wanted to become a doctor. If he had, he thought, he would know what the things were that Ruth was getting ready.

"I'll need your help, Steve," she said to him.

"But I don't know anything about operations."

"I know you don't. But I can't do this by myself. I'll tell you what to do. OK?"

"OK. Sure."

"First, wash your hands. Then put on these rubber gloves."

Steve washed and put on the rubber gloves that Ruth gave him. Then she helped him into a white gown like the one she was wearing. She tied a white piece of cloth around his mouth and nose. She also tied one over his head to cover his hair.

"We're just about ready to begin now," she said.

"I'm not sure *I* am," Don said from where he lay on the table.

"You can still back out of this," Ruth said to him. "In fact, I still think you should."

Don smiled up at her from the table. "I was just kidding. You talked as if I didn't have any say in the matter—like I wasn't even here. Are all you doctors like that?"

Instead of answering him, Ruth put something over his nose. In a few minutes, Don was sleeping.

"Hand me that," Ruth said to Steve. She pointed to a small, sharp knife.

Steve gave it to her. She used it to cut the hair from a small place on Don's head.

"Now give me that other knife."

Steve handed it to her. She took it from him and cut through the skin of Don's head. Blood ran from the cut she had made.

She reached for a square piece of white cloth. She used it to dry up the blood. She cut a small hole in Don's head, and then she placed the computer in the hole she had made. She began to connect the computer's wires to parts of Don's brain.

Her hands moved fast. She seemed to be very sure of what she was doing. Some time later, she told Steve that it was all over. She put a

small white bandage on the side of Don's head. Then she took off her gown and gloves. Steve did the same.

"The computer is just under his skin," she told Steve. "I connected its wires to his brain. Now the computer will work again."

"When will Don wake up?"

"Not for some time yet. And when he does wake up, he'll probably be very weak for a time."

Ruth washed her hands and so did Steve. Then he sat down beside Don. To Steve, the hands of the clock on the wall seemed to stand still. He got up and walked from one end of the operating room to the other. Then he came back and sat down again. Ruth sat down beside him. Both of them watched Don. Don's eyes were still closed.

There was a sound outside the operating room.

"There must be someone out there in the hall," Steve said. He ran to the door. He put his ear against it. He heard the sound again. He opened the door a crack. Then he closed it fast and turned to face Ruth.

"Robots," he whispered, as he locked the door.

Ruth's eyes grew wide. She looked down at Don. Then she said to Steve, "If they come in here. . . ."

"I've locked the door."

Steve looked around the operating room. "Is there any other way out of here?"

Ruth shook her head. "That's the only door."

"Then we're trapped," Steve said.

As he spoke, the handle of the door turned. Then it turned again. One of the robots outside began to pound on the door.

Ruth watched as Steve moved about the room. He seemed to be looking for something.

"What's this?" he asked and pointed to a handle set in the wall.

"That's where we throw our dirty laundry," Ruth said.

"Where does this laundry chute lead?"

"It goes to the bottom of the hospital."

Steve pulled on the handle. He tore the laundry chute's door right out of the wall. Now there was a square hole in the wall where the door had been.

Outside in the hall, the robots still pounded on the door. Their metal hands beat on the door as if it were a drum. The sound hurt Steve's and Ruth's ears.

"You slide down the laundry chute," Steve told Ruth. "Then I'll put Don in the chute. You can catch him. Then I'll slide down the chute."

Ruth said, "No, you go first. I'll stay here with Don."

"But. . . ."

"You go first," Ruth said a second time.

Steve didn't want to. But there was no time to waste. He got into the chute and went down it. He landed in a big pile of dirty laundry. He got up and looked up the chute. He could see Ruth's face far above him.

"Send Don down now," he called up to her. "Take it easy with him. I'll catch him."

He held out his arms. Don came down the chute, and Steve caught him. Don was still not awake. Steve placed him on the floor. He looked up the laundry chute.

"Ruth!" he shouted. "Your turn now."

Ruth started to climb into the laundry chute.

Suddenly, Steve heard a crash. It came from the operating room above.

The door, he thought. The robots have broken down the door. "Ruth!" he yelled.

He saw her pulled back from the chute by the robots. "Ruth!" he yelled again.

She screamed. Her voice sounded like the voice of an animal caught in a trap. But there was nothing he could do to help her. He couldn't climb up the chute. There was just no way for him to get to her.

Suddenly, he saw her in the chute up above. A robot was holding her over its head! The robot threw Ruth down the chute. Steve caught her, feeling sick. He looked down at her. Ruth's eyes were closed. There was blood on her head and in her hair.

He put her down on the floor. He checked—she had no heart beat.

He couldn't seem to think. He was about to give up hope. What could he do now? Ruth was dead, killed by the robots. Don was not awake. The helicar was on the roof of the hospital. And the robots would find him soon. They knew where he was. Then it would be all over.

He let out an angry cry. He needed super-human help. Then the ugly sound of metal against metal met his ears.

A robot came down the laundry chute. Steve grabbed a chair. He hit the robot with it. Once. Twice. The robot broke. Steve stuffed it into the laundry chute.

The broken robot blocked the chute. Now no more robots could slide down and get out.

Steve looked down at Ruth. Then he looked at Don. He couldn't carry both of them. He would have to leave Ruth's body behind. He decided to make a run for it. It was the only thing he could do.

He picked up Don and left the room. He

made his way out of the hospital. Once outside on the street, he looked around. No robots. Good. He began to walk as fast as he could. But Don was very heavy, so he couldn't walk as fast as he wanted to.

He turned a corner and saw two robots coming toward him. He ducked back around the corner. He would hide until the robots were gone.

But his plan didn't work. The two robots turned the corner. They saw Steve. They started after him. But he got away in time. He ducked into a building. He climbed, with Don on his back, up the stairs of the building.

At last, he came out on the roof. Now what, he asked himself. He didn't know the answer. He looked around. The hospital was not far away. There were a few buildings in between.

But between the roofs of the buildings there were wide spaces. He could jump from building to building with no trouble *if* he didn't have to carry Don.

If he didn't have to worry about Don, he could get away. He was sure of it. But he would *not* leave Don to the robots. Then Steve remembered—since this planet was ⅛ the size of

Earth, gravity on the Red World would be less than Earth's.

He backed up. Then he began to run. He jumped.

Steve almost floated to the roof of the next building. He sat down and took a deep breath. Then he got up again. Holding on to Don, who was across his back, he jumped to the next building. He made it. He jumped the next space. And the next. His legs were about to give out.

But there was the hospital! It was the very next building!

Steve took several deep breaths. Then he jumped—and landed on the roof of the hospital. But he was so weak, he fell down. Don's body fell beside him.

For a long time, Steve could only lie there. In his mind was one thought. *Don's helicar.* It wasn't far away.

He had to get to it. He forced himself to get up. He picked up Don and took him to the helicar. He put Don inside. Then he climbed in beside Don and shut the door behind him.

Just then, several robots came out on the roof of the hospital. The sight of them made Steve mad. He thought about Ruth. He thought of what the robots had done to the people of the city. Of what they had done to the city itself.

He raced the motor of the helicar. He flew it up into the sky.

Then he turned it and headed back toward the hospital roof. He flew down fast and hit the group of robots. They fell. But they got up right away. They began to run from the roof.

But Steve was too fast for them. He flew toward them as fast as the helicar would go. This time, when he hit them, he knocked them all off the roof. The robots broke into pieces as they fell.

Only then did he turn the helicar toward the night side of the planet.

"That," he said out loud, "was for you, Ruth."

CHAPTER 6

DON AND THE ROBOTS

Steve flew over the city. Then he turned the helicar around and went back the way he had just come.

When he reached the hospital, he looked down. What he saw made him happy. Down on the street in front of the hospital was a pile of broken metal. Wires lay all over the ground.

What had once been many robots was now nothing but a pile of broken machines. Steve had come back to make sure they had been destroyed.

As Steve flew away from the city toward the night side of the planet, he looked over at Don seated beside him. When Don woke up, he would have to tell him what had just happened. How could he bring himself to do it? If he were in Don's place, he knew how he would feel when he heard about what had happened to the woman he loved. Or did he know?

Steve flew on and soon came to the night side of the planet. Thoughts as black as the planet's night side filled his mind. He almost wished that he had never become an astronaut. If he hadn't, he wouldn't now be faced with having to tell Don that Ruth was dead. Maybe I should have stayed on Earth, he thought. But he knew he wouldn't be happy that way.

He almost laughed at himself. Was he happy now? The answer was—no. He wasn't. Poor Ruth, he thought. Her troubles are over, but Don's are just about to begin.

As the helicar flew through the dark, Don woke up. He opened his eyes and looked around. "Where am I?"

Steve told him. He wished that Don would go back to sleep. He didn't want to tell him about Ruth. But he knew that he would have to tell him.

"Is the operation over?" Don asked.

Steve couldn't hear him very well. Don's voice was low, almost a whisper.

"Yes, it's over," Steve said as the helicar flew through the dark. "The computer is now connected to your brain."

Don touched the bandage on the right side of his head. "I feel . . ." he began. He searched for the right word. Finally, he said, "Different. That's how I feel. Like a different person."

"You *are* different now," Steve said. "You're not just a man now. You know much more than any man or woman. You know what you have always known, of course. But now you have the computer's power."

Was he trying to stop Don from asking the question he didn't want to answer? Was he just killing time?

But then Don looked around the helicar again. He sat up in his seat. "Where's Ruth?"

There it was. The question. Steve said, "She isn't here, Chadrow."

"I can see that. *Where* is she?"

"Let me tell you what happened at the hospital." Steve then told him the whole story. About the robots. About how they broke into the operating room. About the laundry chute. "I caught you when you came down the chute," he said.

"That still doesn't answer my question." Don's voice was as cold as ice. "Where's Ruth? She *is* OK, isn't she?"

Steve couldn't speak, couldn't answer. Don grabbed his arm.

"Tell me where she is!" he shouted.

"I'm sorry, Don. Ruth is dead. The robots killed her."

Don fell back in his seat. He let go of Steve's arm.

"How did it happen?"

Steve told him.

Don said, "You should have let her go down the chute first."

"I wanted her to go first. I *told* her to. But she wouldn't. She didn't want to leave you. So I went down."

"If you had *made* her go first. . . ."

"Don, listen to me. I couldn't change her mind. There was no time to waste. The robots were at the door. She wanted to stay with you. She loved you."

"I loved her." Don whispered. His eyes were wet. "I loved that woman more than I love my life. I can't believe she's dead. I *won't* believe it!" He covered his face with his hands.

Just then, Steve saw the camp fire in front of them. He landed and got out of the helicar. So did Don. The people at the camp crowded around them. When they heard about Ruth, some people cried. They told Don that they were very sorry.

Steve asked Don the question that was on all their minds. "Will you go back to the city with me and stop the robots?"

Don looked at Steve. "*Stop* them?"

Steve thought that Don didn't understand the question.

But then Don said, "Yes, I'll stop them. You can bet your sweet life that I'll stop them."

"Do you feel strong enough now?"

"Let's go," Don said.

"Perhaps you should rest first."

But Don wouldn't rest. He got back into the helicar and looked out at Steve. "You don't have to come. I can do this by myself."

"I'll come, Chadrow," Steve said and got in beside Don.

Before they took off, Steve told the people in the camp that they could now return to the city. By the time they got there, he told them, Don would have the robots under control.

"Under control," Don said and smiled.

The people began to leave the camp. The helicar flew into the sky. When it reached the city, Don landed on the roof of the hospital. Steve followed him down the steps into the hospital. When they got to the laundry room, Don stopped.

Ruth's body lay where Steve had left it.

Don picked her up. He walked past Steve.

"I have to lay her to rest," he said. He left the hospital.

Steve waited for him to return. Time passed. But at last Don came back. A cold fire burned in his eyes.

"I'm ready now," he told Steve.

They left the hospital. As soon as they came out on the street, a robot spotted them. It began to run toward them. Its metal hands reached out for them.

As the robot ran toward them, Don didn't move. All at once, the robot stopped in its tracks. It didn't move again. Its arms reached out into thin air.

"You did it!" Steve shouted. "That robot can't move. Keep it up, Chadrow. Soon their show will be all over."

Don said nothing. Suddenly, the robot blew up. Pieces of metal and broken wires flew through the air.

"Chadrow!" Steve yelled. "Do you know what you are doing, man?"

Don didn't answer him. Instead, he began to walk through the city. Steve could only follow him.

Every time they met a robot, Don blew it up. Steve knew there was no stopping him. He knew that Don didn't just want to control the robots. He wanted to destroy every last one of them.

It took hours. But finally it was all over. Every robot in the city had been destroyed. Only then did Don stop to rest.

"You didn't have to destroy them all," Steve said. "The people need robots. They do most of the work in the city."

Don looked at Steve. "I'm sorry you can't understand why I destroyed them."

Steve was suddenly angry. "That's not fair,

Chadrow. Not at all fair. I *do* understand why you did it. But it would have been better to just control them, not destroy them. Then they could do the work they did before."

"Not these robots," Don said. "I wouldn't trust them. What if I got sick? Or killed? The same thing would happen again. No, the people can get new robots. They can order them from Earth. The new ones are better. They *can't* go out of control." Don began to walk back the way they had come. Steve went with him.

He said, "I have to get in touch with Drake. Where is your signal system?"

Don took him to the signal building.

Steve sent a signal to Ellen. He told her everything that had happened. He said she could do away with the force field now.

When the men came out of the building, all the people were back. They had begun to clean up the city. Steve told Don he had to get back to Voyager. Don walked along with him.

As they walked, Don spoke of his life with Ruth. He showed Steve the building where they had lived together.

"That park over there—see it? We went there a lot. We had many happy times there.

We talked about how nice it would be to bring our baby there."

Steve stopped.

Don looked at him. "Yes, Ruth was going to have a baby. It would have been our first."

"Oh, Don. . . ." Steve's voice broke.

"I want you to know something, Estrada. I want you to know that Ruth and the baby are not dead because of you. I don't blame you. I was wrong to say it the way I did. I know it now."

They walked on. When they reached Voyager, Steve said, "Well, I guess this is goodbye." He held out his hand to Don.

But Don didn't take Steve's hand. He looked back at the city. "There's nothing there for me now. It's all gone. I don't want to stay here now." He stopped for a minute. Then, without looking at Steve, he said, "I'd like to come with you and Ellen."

Steve was taken by surprise.

Don spoke again. "Every place I'd go around here, I'd see Ruth. But she wouldn't be here, Steve. I couldn't stand it. My life here is over. I have to build a new life for myself. You can help me do it."

Steve said, "Come on. Let's both get on board. First we'll cut your hair so you'll feel more comfortable with a space helmet on. Then we all have work to do."

After Ellen and Steve gave Don a haircut, they all took from the ship the things they had brought. They took them to the people in New World City.

Then all three got back on Voyager.

The big jets fired, and the ship climbed into the sky—past the red sun and on toward Galaxy 5.